People Around To...

MEET THE FARMER

By Joyce Jeffries

Gareth Stevens
Publishing

Please visit our website, www.garethstevens.com. For a free color catalog of all our high-quality books, call toll free 1-800-542-2595 or fax 1-877-542-2596.

Library of Congress Cataloging-in-Publication Data

Jeffries, Joyce.
Meet the farmer / by Joyce Jeffries.
  p. cm. — (People around town)
Includes index.
ISBN 978-1-4339-9368-8 (pbk.)
ISBN 978-1-4339-9369-5 (6-pack)
ISBN 978-1-4339-9367-1 (library binding)
1. Farmers—Juvenile literature. 2. Occupations—Juvenile literature. 3. Agriculture—Juvenile literature. I. Jeffries, Joyce. II. Title.
S519.J44 2013
331.7—dc23

First Edition

Published in 2014 by
Gareth Stevens Publishing
111 East 14th Street, Suite 349
New York, NY 10003

Copyright © 2014 Gareth Stevens Publishing

Editor: Ryan Nagelhout
Designer: Nicholas Domiano

Photo credits: Cover, p. 1 Alexander Raths/Shutterstock.com; p. 5 Stockbyte/Thinkstock.com; pp. 7, 9, 11, 13, 17, 19, 24 (tractor, henhouse) iStockphoto/Thinkstock.com; p. 15 Joy Brown/Shutterstock.com; p. 21 Nancy Honey/Cultura/Getty Images; pp. 23, 24 (tilapia) Greg Vaughn/Perspectives/Getty Images.

All rights reserved. No part of this book may be reproduced in any form without permission in writing from the publisher, except by a reviewer.

Printed in the United States of America

CPSIA compliance information: Batch #CS13GS: For further information contact Gareth Stevens, New York, New York at 1-800-542-2595.

Contents

Friendly Farmer 4

Big Tools 8

Plants and Animals 10

Words to Know 24

Index 24

Farmers feed your family!

5

They live off the land.

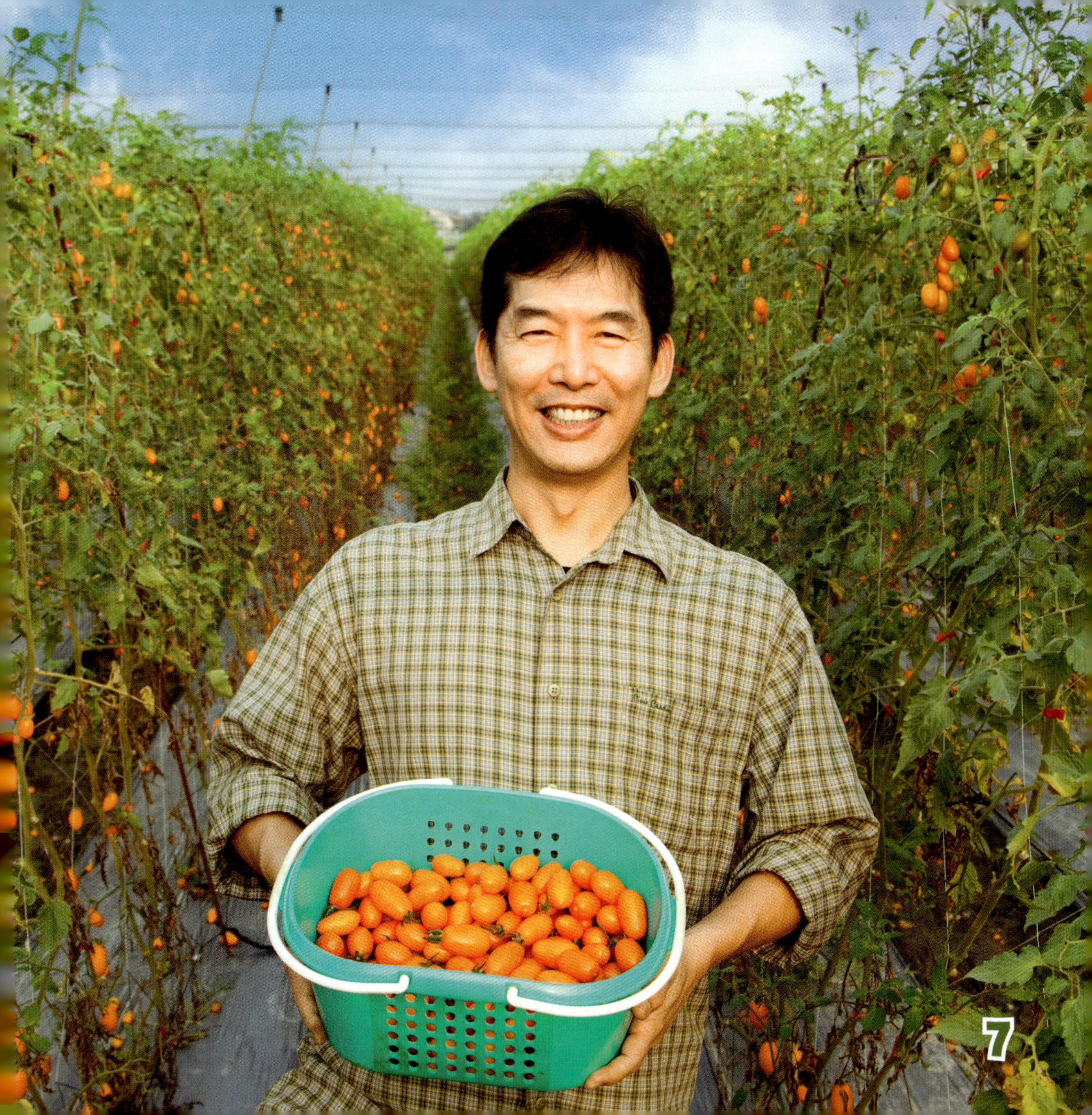

A big machine helps
them plant seeds.
This is called a tractor.

9

They grow plants like wheat.

11

They take care
of animals.

13

Their cows and goats give us milk!

15

Dogs are used to herd sheep.

17

Farmers raise horses.
You can ride horses
on a farm!

19

Chickens get their own home. This is called a henhouse.

21

Tilapia are raised on fish farms.

23

Harris County Public Library
Houston, Texas

Words to Know

henhouse tilapia tractor

Index

fish farms 22

tractor 8

milk 14

wheat 10